PRAIRIE TOWN

BONNIE and ARTHUR GEISERT

HOUGHTON MIFFLIN COMPANY BOSTON
1 9 9 8

307.72
Gei

For Norma, June, Gloria, Larry, Donna, and their families

Walter Lorraine 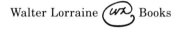 Books

Text copyright © 1998 by Bonnie Geisert
Illustrations copyright © 1998 by Arthur Geisert

Library of Congress Cataloging-in-Publication Data
Geisert, Bonnie.
    Prairie town / Bonnie and Arthur Geisert.
        p.   cm.
    Summary: Describes a year in the life of a prairie town including
the effect of seasons and of economics on the ebb and flow of this
agricultural community.
    ISBN 0-395-85907-7
    1. Cities and towns — Middle West — Juvenile literature.
2. Prairies — Middle West — Juvenile literature.   3. Country life —
Middle West — Juvenile literature.   4. Seasons — Middle West —
Juvenile literature.   [1. Cities and towns.   2. Prairies.
3. Middle West.   4. Country life.   5. Seasons.]   I. Geisert,
Arthur.   II. Title.
HT123.5.M53G45   1998
307.72'0978 — dc21   97-40049
                                                                       CIP
                                                                        AC

Printed in the United States of America
HOR   10   9   8   7   6   5   4   3   2   1

PRAIRIE TOWN

During the early 1900s, railroad companies laid tracks across America's open land. In fields of grass beside the new tracks, surveyors planted their stakes and the prairie towns grew. The towns prospered amid the bounty of wheat fields, and grain elevators dominated the skyline.

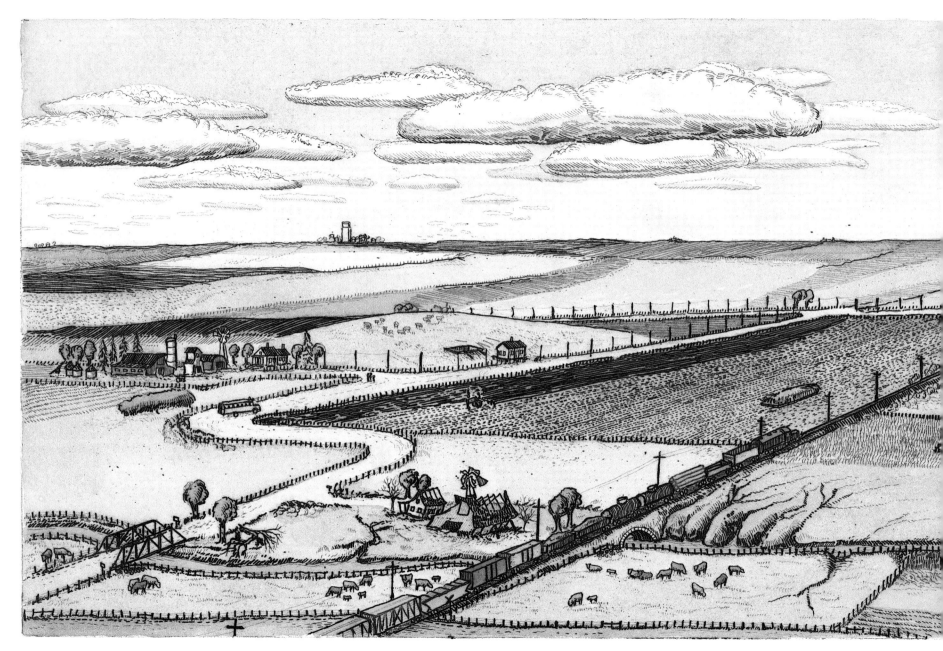

In the spring, a warm wind blows over the prairie and through the town.

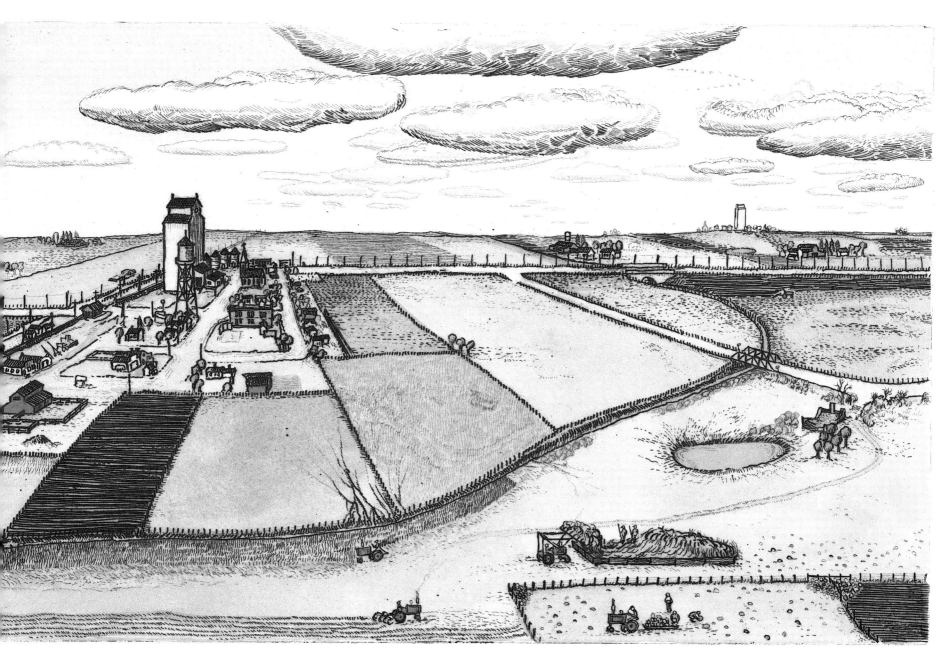

Another growing season has begun. Farmers are busy planting crops and making hay.

The sights, sounds, and activities of spring are everywhere, in the school and in
the churches, homes, and businesses built along streets laid out on a grid.

The grain elevator, skyscraper of the prairie, stands on a prized lot beside the railroad tracks.

The town and its farm neighbors are economic and social partners.
They provide goods and services for each other.

The back yard is a favorite place where families extend their work and play.

As spring warms into summer, the trees, grass, and gardens mature. The corn grows fast. And children no longer merely dream of summer.

Change is always taking place. Some changes are very visible. Others affect only a few.

At the grain elevator, there is a lull in business before the harvest season.
Workers have time to watch the comings and goings of others.

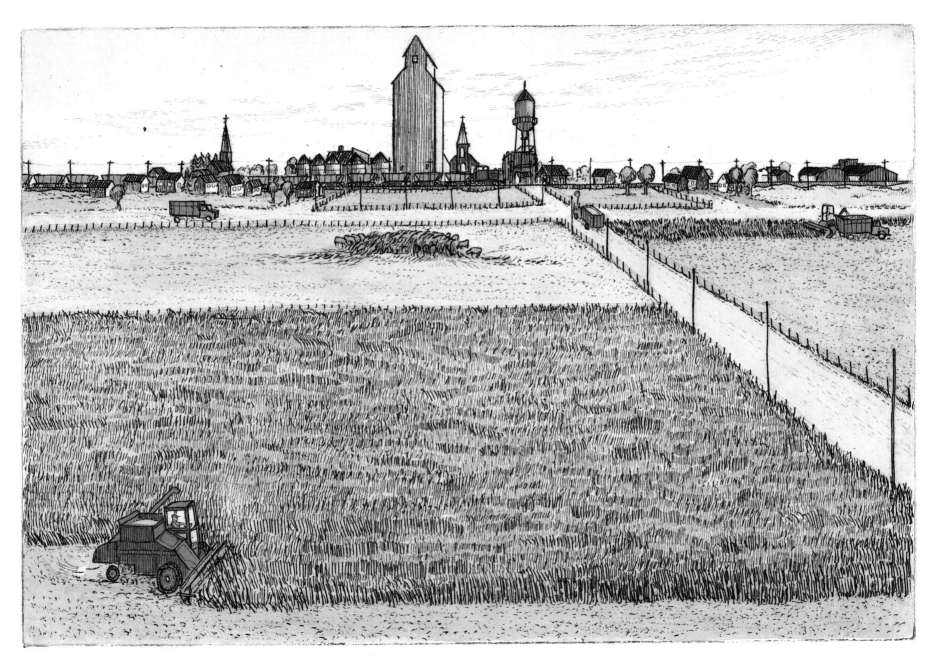

In midsummer, the grain ripens and the harvest machines swing into full gear on the farms. The grain elevator in town becomes a busy place.

Trucks haul load after load of grain to the elevator during the long summer days of harvest.

Trains carry grain to faraway markets, making room for more grain in the elevator.

On beautiful days, the whole town is the children's playground. But weather can change, and the sky is watched anxiously when clouds appear.

Life is affected by the weather. A town's business depends on the farmers' good fortune.
Rain can insure a good crop. A hailstorm, drought, or tornado can destroy it.

When a carnival comes to town, there's excitement in the air. Circus animals, carnival people in costumes, and whirling rides are a welcome change in routine.

One day each week, the sounds of livestock can be heard from their pens at the sale barn. Farmers bring animals to sell, and buyers bid at a weekly auction.

Shorter days and cooler temperatures trigger fall frosts. Leaves fall from the trees. In the corn fields, ears mature on dry stalks under an uninterrupted sky.

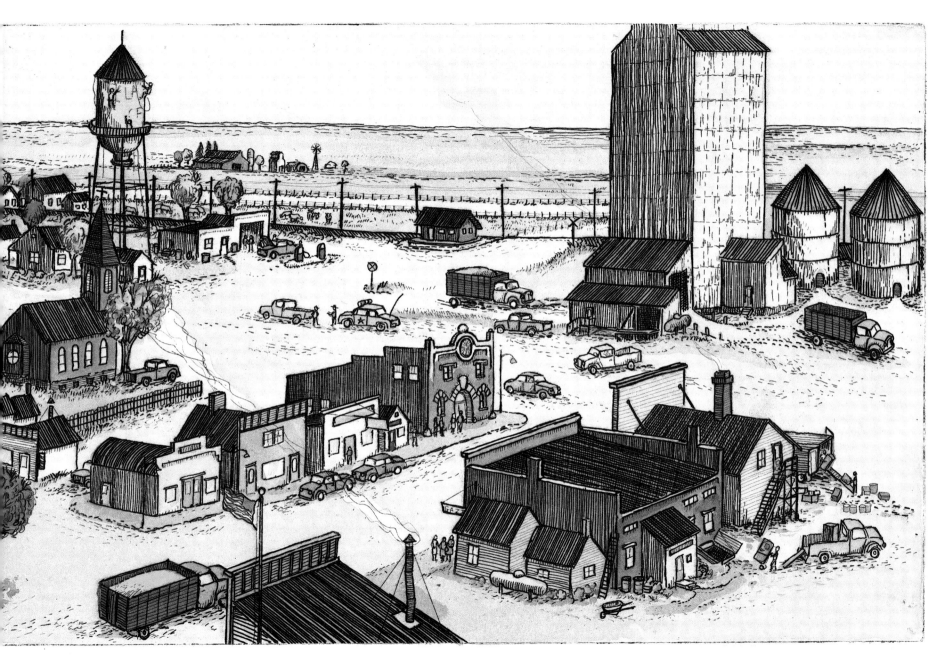

School is back in session, and farm children swell the population during the day.
At night, activities such as sports and music bring friends and families together.

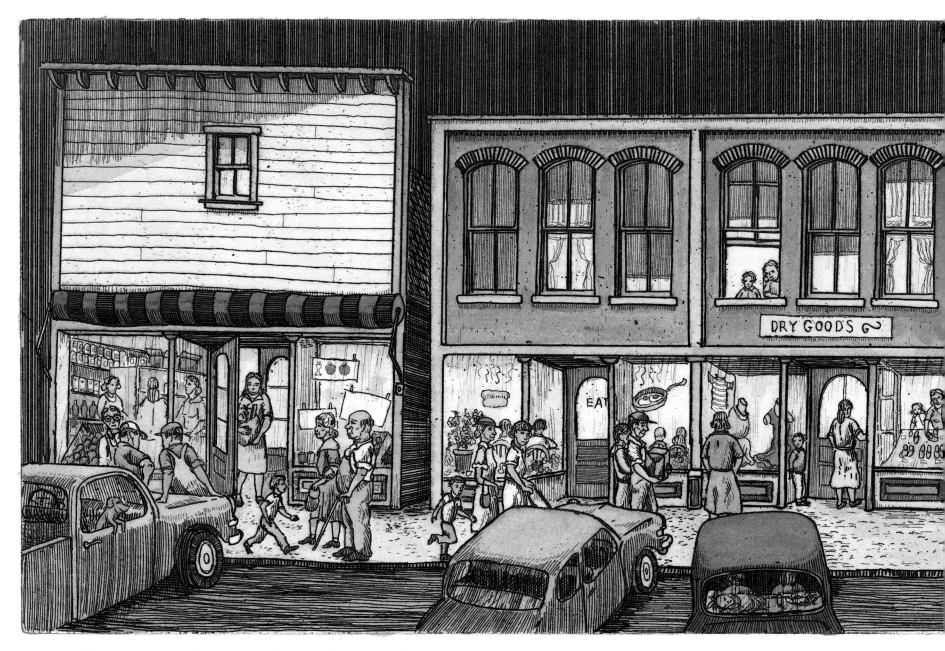

One night each week, often Friday or Saturday, is a big night in town.
Businesses stay open and people come to shop and visit.

Everyone knows everyone else's name. The people in and around the town call it their "home town."

Winter soon follows fall. Arctic air and snow bring a blizzard to the town.
Snow covers the streets and yards and is blown horizontally through the air.

People stay in their homes. Travel is difficult and vehicles are stranded.
The wind sweeps the snow into high drifts against buildings and fences.

When the wind dies down, the cold night air carries the howls of coyotes.

Most people wait until morning to shovel, but the snowplows start as soon as the drivers can see.

Shoveling out is long, hard work. School is canceled if the roads are blocked, and the "snow day" is a winter holiday for the children.

The stores are busy after people emerge from snowbound homes—especially the grocery store.

Winter eventually loses its fury. A warmer wind and the meadowlarks' songs herald the return of spring to the prairie town.

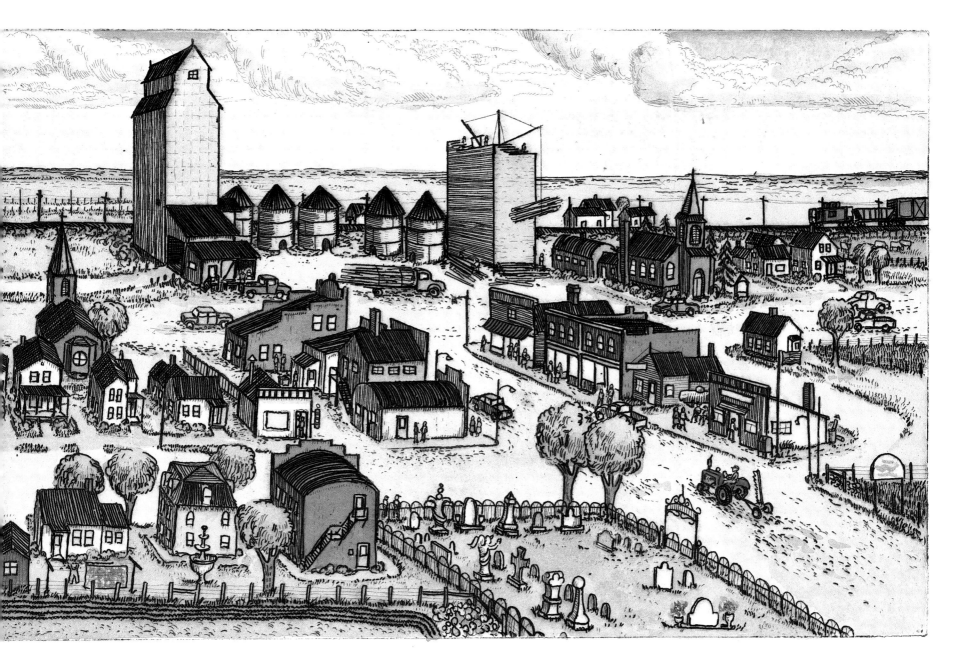

The fragrance of new growth is in the air. Spring work fills the days.

A year has passed in the prairie town. Stories of everyday life, continuing from season to season, can be seen in the illustrations. The stories tell of people at work and play.

People are busy repairing and maintaining homes, yards, businesses, and services. The post office chimney, a fence, fire trucks, a back yard barn, birdbaths, and dying trees are tended. A junk-filled yard is finally cleaned up.

New construction takes place at the house that burned and at the surveyed site of the second grain elevator. A treehouse, more visible in fall, is made bigger in summer. A country house is moved to town. A new family moves into a house that sold. More playground equipment was added in the schoolyard.

A lumber spill, a hole in a fishing boat, a runaway cow on sale day, a traffic ticket, and graffiti on a newly painted water tower are aggravations that cause extra work.

The prairie town experienced the joy of a wedding and the sorrow of death in this year. There was bounty in the grain fields and the pumpkin patch. And one back yard is filled with new spring puppies.